Innocent Promise
Harper Ray

Designer: Artista Grafico

Editor: Jenn Maryk

Visit my website at www.authorharperray.com

Printed in the United States of America

First Printing: May 25, 2024

Author's Note
Trigger Warning

This book is labeled 'Dark' for a reason. It has graphic depictions of themes that some may find triggering such as violence, and explicit sexual scenes.

Explicit language is written throughout the book. If you're sensitive to these types of words, DO NOT READ!

Due to the violent nature, sexual themes, and detailed graphic depictions of certain scenes, it is recommended for readers aged 18+ who are not sensitive to such material.

Table of Contents

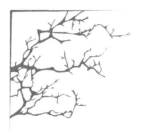

Prologue

P*resent Day*

Mercy

"Mercy!" I knew my friend was calling me, but I couldn't look away from the figure blocking my path. His sharp blue eyes were locked on mine. It seemed like he was so far away, yet he was standing right in front of me. The world stood still as I looked deeply into his eyes. I sucked in a sharp breath when he moved closer.

"Mercy, what's going on?" I knew Chloe couldn't see what I could. It was a gift I'd rather soon deny than admit, but the man in front of me had that same endearing, yet intense presence he had when we first met two years ago. I shook my head to clear it, but when I opened my eyes again, he was still standing there, in all his glory, while his eyes seared into my soul.

Cian Knight.

That was his name. He was the stranger who took my breath away that night and made me feel things I never wanted to forget. He had called to my soul in a way that no other man ever did before. It sounded crazy, and I knew it was crazy, but he had set my heart, soul, and body on fire that night.

If only I'd known then how much pain he would put me through when he left me behind that night.

After all, Cian Knight was no ordinary man.

No, Cian Knight was a *vampire*.

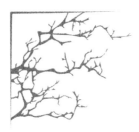

Chapter One

T *wo Years Ago...*

Mercy

"Has anyone ever told you how beautiful you are?"

I startled, and the drink in my hand sloshed over the side. I eagerly set it down on the table before I made the mistake of dropping the glass on the floor. When I looked up, my breath caught. The man's intense blue stare held me captive. He easily towered over my 5'4 stature with his tall six foot frame. Not only was he tall, but he was extremely intimidating.

He looked like a linebacker. His shoulders were broad, and his arm muscles were strong and almost bulged out beneath his red shirt. His midnight hair was a little long, a bit too long for my taste, where the ends curled at the base of his neck, but all in all, he was utterly breathtaking. From his long, straight nose down to his full lips and a chin that had one single dimple in the middle of it, the guy was a complete sight for sore eyes.

My eyes continued to roam over him, noting the scruff on his chin and around his mouth to the look of pure amusement in his gaze when mine returned. My face immediately turned a dark shade of crimson when I realized I was caught in the act.

I shook my head to clear it. "I'm sorry, what did you say?"

He grinned, and a mouth full of white teeth was revealed. "I asked if anyone has ever told you how beautiful you are."

My brows furrowed together. Beautiful? Me? Was he crazy?

I mean sure, I knew I had semi-decent looks, but no guy as hot as him had ever given me the time of day. I had long auburn hair that went past my shoulders and almost reached the base of my ass, and emerald green eyes that almost looked like a pukish green every time I looked in the mirror. My nose was small and made me look like a pixie, and my lips were so thin they hardly looked like I had any. Maybe I was over-exaggerating, but damn, I felt like a lopsided freak half the time, especially when I was around my best friend Chloe.

Now she was beautiful. I would never tell her that though, because her ego was already through the roof. I swear, she was more like a guy sometimes than an actual woman.

I realized I'd gone quiet again as the man was awaiting my answer, so I politely smiled and shook my head. I placed my hands in my lap as he continued to study me. To be honest, it was a little weird how he looked at me so intently. If he wasn't as hot as he was, it probably would've been creepy.

He gestured to the seat in front of me. "Do you mind if I join you?"

Something that felt like a bunch of nervous butterflies swarmed my stomach. *Why was I nervous all of a sudden?* I was fine, minding my own business, laughing as Chloe tried to put moves on the dance floor but failed miserably. Chloe was many things, but a dancer definitely wasn't one of them. Thankfully, that was one of my talents, if not my only talent. I was doing fine on my own, but then he had to come over here, trying to talk to me and making me all nervous and shit.

"So, what's your story, Little Red?" It sounded like he had a hint of an accent, but I had no idea what kind of accent it was. Wait a minute, did he just call me Little Red? My brows turned inward, and I frowned.

"Little Red?" I asked. He made me sound like Little Red Riding Hood. While I loved the story as a kid, I was no little red riding hood. That was for damn sure. I'd seen way too much in my lifetime to be counted as an innocent bystander.

A deep, throaty chuckle rumbled from his chest as he laughed. It was quite a sight. "Well, you have red hair, but beyond that, you seem like a little spitfire, so that's the nickname I've given you."

I rolled my eyes and reached for my drink. The coconut oozed down my throat as I took as many sips as I could before I returned my narrowed gaze to him. "Fine, two can play that game. Linebacker."

His thick brows rose and for a minute he scowled until his features relaxed and he belted out a laugh. "Touché Little Red."

"Ugh. Are you going to ask me my real name, or are we going to sit here going back and forth with different nicknames, because trust me, I'd have you beat."

He smirked. "Oh really? So then I guess you wouldn't mind a little bet then, would you?"

I crossed my arms over my chest. "That depends. What kind of bet are you thinking about?"

He leaned back and put his arms on the back of the booth. "I want to see how many nicknames you have in your vocabulary. If I win, you come back to my place with me. If you win, you can ask for anything you want."

My eyes widened briefly, then I thought about how I could use this to my advantage. Wait, did he just say go back to his place?

My body instantly heated up from the thought of going back to his place. Maybe that wouldn't be so bad, would it?

His blue eyes sparkled with mischief. The bastard honestly thought he had it in the bag, but he was mistaken. I was pretty much a badass when it came to this shit. My lips lifted at the corners.

I stuck out my hand. "Deal."

The bastard wouldn't know what hit him.

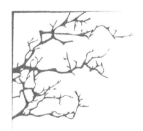

Chapter Two

*C*ian

My God, she was breathtaking.

She was a craving that I so desperately wanted to taste. Her delectable long neck was exposed to me, and her strawberry scent drove me mad. My hands clenched into fists on the back of the booth when she smiled at me.

The only thing that was on my mind was driving into her and biting into her exposed neck. I would do anything to bring her back to my place. Even if it meant playing a silly little game to get her to trust me.

Fuck.

Before I became a vampire, I was a normal, living, breathing human. Just like her. Now, it seemed that I was consumed with the idea of draining the human dry so I could fit my needs, but with her, it was somehow different. There wasn't that hunger I had with most humans; instead it was a lust unlike anything I've ever experienced before.

When I was a human, I was a bit of a man whore. Hell, I still was. But I somehow calmed down in that sense and became more of a blood whore who wanted nothing but the taste of their succulent blood on my lips.

I wanted to taste her. I wanted to drive my cock into her aching, wet pussy when I bit into her. My fangs started coming out and I knew I needed to hurry this up so I could bury myself into her and move on. Because that's what I really wanted.

To move on. Right now though, I could use a good distraction from the shit that was my life.

Nobody told me how fucking hard it would be to become a vampire. No, my fucking sister left that part out when she turned me. You see, it was a coming of age thing in my family. Once a human turned a certain age, they would be turned by one of their family members to keep the family bloodline going. Only with my family, there was a bit more responsibility than just that.

The difference between my family and me though, was I didn't want this. Like Little Red said, I looked like a linebacker. Hell, I was one. I lived and breathed football back in my human days, but now I had a responsibility to the family. Find my mate, bring her home and become King and Queen of the Sanguine Kingdom. I didn't want this responsibility. I hated my family right now for putting this bullshit on my shoulders. I was twenty-five, and I would forever remain that age for the rest of my days. Which, unless I was killed, would be eternity.

So, my thought process? Be a bachelor as long as I fucking could, but the way Little Red was looking at me right now, while she bit her lip? Undid me to my fucking core. She would be the death of me, and I vowed to never let that happen. I wasn't ready to settle down and I sure as shit wasn't ready to be King. My father was a dick and I didn't want to end up being the heartless, soulless bastard he was. But reigning over the Sanguine turned you into that.

It happened to him, and it happened to my sister. Somehow though, my mother stayed strong enough for all of us and remained as human as she could. She was graceful, kind and completely and one hundred percent a "good" vampire. I tried to be, but most times, I failed her. More often than not, I couldn't control my thirst and would end up draining the human dry. It was a work in progress and I was getting better, but I was still a young vampire. My older sister turned before me and therefore had much more experience than I had and honestly wished it was her that could bear all this weight on her shoulders.

I was brought back from my thoughts when her sweet and sexy voice interrupted them. "So, Linebacker, are we going to do this bet or not?"

I looked in her emerald eyes and saw the mischief there, but I also noticed the lack of confidence in her gaze. I leaned forward and decided to poke her further. "What's the matter, Little Red? Are you scared?"

She scoffed. "Not at all. I would like to know your real name though, so we can move past this nonsense."

I smirked. "See if you can figure it out."

She pursed her lips and went into deep thought. "Liam?"

I made a face. "Hell no!"

She tilted her head back and laughed. "What's wrong with Liam?"

"That sounds like a pussy name, Little Red. Try again." I noticed a waitress headed our way. I reached for her glass and lifted it in the air to signal for her to bring another one. The blonde nodded and went in the other direction. Maybe I should've gotten something, but the only thing I thirsted for was Little Red's sweet blood on my lips. I set the glass down when Red said another name.

"I'm sorry, what was that?"

She rolled her eyes and huffed. "I said, Cade, Mason, Jackson, Jason, Cole, and Tate. Am I getting close?"

I grinned. "You were closer when you were on the names that start with C."

She opened her mouth to say something else, but someone interrupted us. "Damn girl, who is this fine ass specimen that you have sitting with you?"

A girl with short black hair scooted into the booth, making Red move over. While this woman had a nice set of tits to look at, the rest of her dulled in comparison to Red.

Red flushed a shade of crimson, and opened her mouth. "I don't know. Linebacker meet Chloe. Chloe, meet Linebacker."

Chloe raised a perfectly manicured black brow. "Linebacker?"

I smirked and pointed to Red. "She hasn't figured out my name yet."

Red scoffed. "HE hasn't figured out my name yet either! So we've resulted to calling each other nicknames, hence Linebacker."

Chloe looked wildly amused by the entire conversation. "Oh really? And what do you call her? Her name is Mercy, by the way."

Mercy. That name seemed to fit her perfectly.

"Chloe! Dammit!"

Chloe shrugged her shoulders. "Live a little, Merc. I'm going to go get a drink, don't have too much fun without me!"

Mercy mumbled under her breath something that sounded like traitor. I grinned.

She glared. "What are you grinning at?"

I shrugged when the waitress brought her another drink. I grinned at how damn adorable she was, but I wasn't about to tell her that.

Mercy brought the glass to her lips, and as she swallowed, the lump in her throat moved, bringing my thirst back in full force. I was starting to get antsy, and impatient.

If I didn't have her in the next few minutes, I was going to go crazy. I sighed and put a hand through my hair. It was now or never. Time to put on the charm.

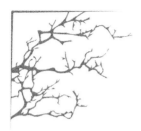

Chapter Three

M*ercy*

Linebacker stood up with a pained look on his face. I set the glass down. "Where are you going?"

His hands clenched at his sides before he quickly moved into the spot that was recently taken by Chloe. He moved so quickly, that my breath was robbed. How did he do that?

I knew my eyes were wide when his returned to mine. He placed an arm on the booth behind me and another on the table in front of us. "I'm not going anywhere, Little Red."

I rolled my eyes. "You know my name now; you can stop calling me that."

He leaned over, encasing me in his musky scent and looked me deep in the eyes. Goosebumps spread on my arms when I felt his fingers lightly touch my skin. My eyes briefly closed.

"I like your nickname, don't you?"

He continued to rub his fingers over my skin, softly spreading tingles of pleasure racing through me. His breath touched the base of my neck when he leaned over and whispered in my ear. "You are so goddamn perfect, Red. I want to taste you."

A sound escaped my mouth, probably more of a whimper, but that sounded incredible coming from his mouth. "I still don't know your name," I whispered.

His lips touched my ear and I had to hold on to the table. "Cian. My name is Cian Knight."

I moaned when he nibbled on my ear. Even from just those simple touches, he ignited my body on fire.

He moved closer, firmly placing his hand on my back, bringing me closer to him.

We were in a loud and noisy bar called Jaspers, but I couldn't seem to give a fuck. All I wanted was him on me and inside of me.

His lips trailed down to my neck, nibbling and sucking and as he did that, I brought my fingers to his midnight hair and held on for dear life. I wanted him to kiss me, to devour me right there in that bar, but he was taking his sweet time. As if he were enjoying tasting my skin between his lips.

I swear, his touch felt different than that of any other man I'd been with. Not that I'd been with many, but I did know that he made me feel alive where others had me constricted, and unable to be myself when it came to my sexual desires.

I opened my eyes when I saw movement. I thought it was someone coming over to the table, but instead it was his hand leaving the table and reaching down to the one place I wanted his fingers to go.

He trailed his fingers down my white tank top and to the top of my shorts where he played with the button for a minute. My stomach quivered at his touch when he opened the button and gently slid down the zipper.

"Fuck, Cian." I hissed through my lips.

He grinned against my neck and continued his perusal. His fingers went past the waistband of my shorts and dipped inside my underwear where he played with my slick folds. I started moving against his fingers, wishing that he would just stick one up there already. We were in a public place, but I didn't seem to give a flying fuck at the moment who was watching the show.

My fingers tightened in his hair, and my eyes rolled to the back of my head. Fuck, this felt so amazing, I didn't want him to stop.

His mouth lifted from my neck, and his fingers left my shorts as he grasped my chin in his hands. Our eyes met for a brief moment before he lowered his lips and devoured mine. This was a whole other feeling of pleasure.

"Holy hell, you two. You might need to take this somewhere else. You're putting on a show for the entire bar."

It felt like cold water splashed over me when I heard Chloe's voice. I opened my eyes when Cian released me, and I moved as far away from him as I could. What the hell was wrong with me? I never, ever acted like that. Especially when in public. It was like he had some kind of spell over me.

She slid on the other side of the booth while Cian and I tried to regain our composure. I quickly buttoned up my shorts and when I looked around, I noticed several eyes on me. Shit.

I heard Chloe snicker and I glared at her. She shrugged. "What? You put on a pretty damn good show, Merc." My cheeks heated and I knew I was as red as an apple.

I glanced at Cian, but he didn't even look at me. His fingers were curled into fists. I placed a hand on his shoulder and he flinched. I immediately removed it.

I sank back into the booth wishing I could disappear. How embarrassing. He wanted me, but now that he knew people were watching he wanted nothing to do with me. Plus, what if this got out around campus? I would be screwed.

Finally, Cian moved. It wasn't the move I was hoping for, but I guess whatever weird reality I was in before was officially over. He stood from the booth, hands curled at his sides. He seemed to be breathing heavily. I wasn't sure what was going on with him or if I had worked him over that much, but I figured it was the latter.

I moved out of the shadows of the booth and went to address Chloe, when a hand appeared in front of me. My eyes moved up to see Cian's heated stare penetrating through me. The offer was clear, the question was did I want to accept?

I heard someone clear their throat, and my gaze returned to Chloe. She nodded her head in Cian's direction and nodded up and down enthusiastically. My eyes once again met Cian's, and for a moment, it seemed like he was persuading me to go with his eyes. Something deep and dark was rooted in the depths and ever so slowly, I put my hand in his.

He lifted me out of the seat, and the next thing I knew, we had left the bar and headed back to his place.

Chapter Four

*C*ian

This woman was driving me insane. I couldn't figure out what it was about her, but she drove me to the brink of insanity. Her soft skin, her supple lips, and her intoxicating scent all made me want to push her against the wall and fuck her until we were both passed out. As crazy as it was, her blood didn't matter to me anymore. We'd only known each other for maybe a couple of hours at most, but there was something about her that made me want more than I was willing to take.

Something deep in my core was calling out to her. When she willingly accepted my hand, I knew that when I took her back to my place, I would show her exactly who she was dealing with and make sure that her pleasure knew no bounds.

The biggest question of all though, was could I keep myself from biting her and tasting her?

The drive back to my place seemed to blur. We were at the bar in one second, and the next we were pulling into my drive. The dark one story house stared back at us as I turned off the car. The house was given to me by my parents in hopes that I would find my mate and bring her back home to continue on the tradition and take on the responsibilities I needed to face.

My jaw ticked and my fingers clenched around the steering wheel when I thought about going back home. Truth was, I didn't want to go home. I liked it here. My home Carpathia, was a region of Romania that the vampire king, Roman Slovak, an ancestor of mine, claimed as the Sanguine.

Long ago, he put a protective barrier around it, encasing the kingdom in darkness. There were several myths about vampires, and one of those myths was that we couldn't go out in sunlight. Truthfully, we could go out in sunlight and have no issues, but, as vampires, we preferred the darkness and therefore, my kingdom was covered in darkness and only had one day out of the year where it would be covered in light. Most of us though, preferred to pretend that day didn't exist.

I was brought out of my thoughts when I heard Red's sweet voice. "Are you alright?"

My eyes moved to hers, and there was concern written all over her face. I smiled, but it came out as more of a grimace. I knew she could tell that my thoughts were somewhere else, but I tried my best to shake off those thoughts and focus on her.

I placed my hand on hers and nodded to the house. "Let's go."

I took the key from the ignition and opened the door. As soon as I got out of the car, I used my powers to flash over to her side and open the door. She didn't seem to notice and just replied with a small thank-you, and got out of the car. Once she was out, I closed the door and pushed her against the car.

Her breathing went ragged when I placed both hands on her hips and moved in closer. My cock sprung to life when it came into contact with her heated core. She released a heavy moan, and her eyes rolled back as I continued to dry hump her against the car. I tangled my fingers in her hair and brought her lips to mine.

The moon was out, but other than the light radiating from it, the night was pitch black. I could've fucked her right here in the driveway, but I knew that was no way to treat her. This woman needed a bed, and to be pleased all night long. I moved my tongue into her mouth and groaned when I tasted the remaining coconut from her drink.

I pulled away and rested my forehead against hers. I needed to do something about this hunger, this inexplicable craving to have her moving underneath me. I opened my eyes, looked into hers and made a promise.

"When we get inside, I am going to fuck you like you've never been fucked before. That's a promise, Little Red."

She let out a breathy moan and giggled. "I hope one day you'll drop that silly nickname."

I smirked. Yeah, not fucking happening. I took her hand in mine and led her up the driveway and through the garage door. When we got inside, I turned on the kitchen lights and went to the fridge. "Do you want something to drink?"

I reached for the bottle that had donated human blood in it but was disguised as a wine bottle. I put the bottle on the counter and went in search of two glasses.

Mercy cleared her throat. "Can I have some water, please?"

I nodded and opened the fridge once more to grab her a bottle of water. I handed it over to her and watched as she opened the cap and started chugging down sip after sip. Her throat bobbed up and down and the movement only made me realize how much hungrier for her than I was five minutes ago. I opened the cork of the wine bottle and poured some of the drink into a glass. As I set the bottle back down, my eyes met hers.

I raised the glass to her. "You want some?"

Maybe it was a stupid idea, and granted, it was. I shouldn't be offering blood to a human, but I was always told that a vampire's future mate wouldn't be appalled by the drink like most humans would. It was one of the many signs that meant they would be willing to change into a vampire to continue their life bound to you. I always thought it was utterly ridiculous, but now, I'll admit, I was a bit curious.

She shook her head. "No thanks, I'm still feeling the previous two drinks I had."

My brows turned inward. "You a lightweight?"

She scowled. "No, I can handle my liquor." She shrugged. "I just don't drink that often, so I'm a little bit tipsy."

I chuckled and took a long drink. The cold blood flowed down my lungs easily. Normally, most vampires hated their blood cold if they stored it, but I didn't mind too much, I knew I would have the real thing soon enough. I set the drink down. "You are a lightweight, Little Red. That's what it means when you can't hold your liquor after two minutes."

She stuck her tongue out at me. I shook my head. She was damn adorable. I moved around the counter and took the water bottle from her hands. I placed it on the kitchen table that was across the bartop and grabbed her hand.

Enough of this. It was time to devour her.

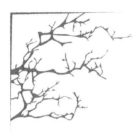

Chapter Five

Mercy

His bedroom was incredible. Heck, the whole house from what I could see, was incredible. There was a king sized bed that was placed in the middle of the room, with a satin red comforter, the base of the bed was black and the rest of the furniture matched the bed. On either side of the bed there were two large windows that allowed the moon's light to bleed through the room.

Cian released my hand and padded across the room to let the curtains fall down the windows so we were encased in darkness. A few minutes later, almost with a click of his fingers it seemed, the bedroom was lit in candlelight. It was a breathtaking sight.

But when his blue eyes met mine as he reached down to lift his shirt over his head, I was once again stunned into silence. The man was a God. He almost didn't seem real. His chest glistened in the candlelight, and I knew that sounded fucking stupid, but he was perfect.

My fingers itched to touch his muscular chest. Slowly, I made my way over to him. The heels I was wearing, per Chloe's request, were becoming all that more difficult to walk in. I was trying to look sexy as I swayed my hips back and forth, but I knew I looked ridiculous. Cian's eyes never left mine though. They started to venture up and down my body and when they stayed on the rise and fall of my breasts, the room became all that much hotter.

I needed him to devour me.

I needed him to fuck me senseless. I wasn't normally this free with my body and my desires, but with him, I didn't seem to care. I wanted to be bare for him. I wanted to spread myself open for him and let him take advantage of me. I wanted him to play me like a goddamn string on a guitar.

Once I stood right in front of him, I placed my hand on his chest. Ever so gently, I used my fingers to trace over the outlines of his chest. When my fingers moved to the button on his jeans, he quivered under my touch. I smiled knowing that I had the same effect on him that he had on me.

Slowly, I unbuttoned his pants. I slid the zipper down, until it couldn't go anywhere else. I stopped short when his fingers went to the bottom of my tank. His fingers slid underneath my shirt and he gently rubbed them over my skin. My eyes closed of their own accord as I enjoyed the feel of his touch.

His fingers went to the back of my bra and undid the clasp leaving it open and just sitting there until he was ready to take it off. My eyes opened and met his gaze once his fingers went back to the bottom of my shirt. I helped him slide it over my chest, taking the bra along with it. My nipples puckered up when they met the cold air.

The anticipation of his next move left me breathless.

His eyes darkened when they zeroed in on my breasts. I stood taller, so my breasts were lifted, but I still paled in comparison to his height. His left hand reached up to grab one of my breasts, while his right hand still remained on my back.

I grunted when he pulled me against him. His hardened cock rubbed against my ass in his pants, straining and wanting desperately to come out and play. His right hand laid flat against my back, kind of like a support system, when his hand left my breast and pushed down on my chest, making me arch backwards. I was in a very awkward position but I couldn't seem to care when finally, his mouth latched onto my nipple. My pussy grew wet with each passing second. His tongue began to lick and his lips sucked my nipple through his teeth as he bit down, hard.

I cried out, trying to move against him, wanting so desperately for him to ravish me right there, but his right hand remained firm on my back, making it impossible to move. His left hand went to my other breast and started to massage it, and that only made me moan more.

It felt so amazing what he was doing to me and I wanted to return the favor. After he was done licking and sucking on one breast, he moved to the other and gave it the same attention. "Cian," I whispered. I wanted him to keep going, but I wanted something else. I craved something more.

He stopped what he was doing and met my gaze. Whatever he saw must have done the trick because he pulled me back up to a standing position. His fingers went to the top of my shorts, but I removed his hands and sank to my knees in front of him.

I looked up at him, and saw his eyes darkened. He wanted me on my knees just as much as I wanted to be there. My fingers moved to his jeans, but he beat me to it. He hurriedly had them off. I grabbed one of my breasts and started massaging it as I waited patiently for him to take off his underwear.

His cock sprung free and oh my, it was magnificent. It was big, and it was hard. It had a piercing on the tip, and my tongue touched the roof of my mouth as I had the urge to play with it. His cock was one hundred percent ready for me. I looked up to him, as I placed my hand on him. My eyes held promise as I bent over and took him into my mouth. He sucked in a sharp breath when my mouth closed over him.

He growled as my head moved back and forth while my hand continued to stroke him. His fingers tightened in my hair, and I knew he was so close to losing control. I was ripped away from him and thrown on the bed. His greedy eyes roamed over my body, and with a force I'd never seen anyone have, he had my shorts and underwear ripped free of my body.

He lifted my hips in the air and stuck his tongue deep inside me. I cried out in pleasure, not caring if the whole world could hear what he was doing to me. He licked and sucked, and then not even giving me a minute to breathe, he put two fingers inside me. He moved them in and out of my soaking wet pussy, and my hips rocked to the rhythm.

The bed was soft and comfortable, but I didn't even have a minute to process because spots invaded my vision and my hips bucked as I came down from the incredible high I was on. He removed his fingers and did something that was the hottest thing I'd ever seen in my life.

He licked his fingers and then moved his hand to the base of his cock so he could stroke and watch me come down from my orgasm. Watching him stroke himself like that only turned me on more. I wanted him in me. Consuming me. I moved my fingers to my folds and started to play with my lips. His eyes darkened even more.

His hand left his cock as he hovered over me and claimed my lips in a deep kiss. He plunged into me in the next second, and my eyes widened in shock from the feel of him completely consuming me. He laid there for a minute, just kissing me and giving my core time to adjust, but then he started to move.

My legs wrapped around his waist, allowing him to go deeper. I moaned, and he grunted as he continued to thrust deeper and harder with each stroke. I moved my lips to his ear and whispered, "Fuck me harder. Cian, fuck me deeper."

That gave him the push he needed. I was on my back, and in the next moment, he had turned me around on my knees with my ass facing up in the air. He pushed my head down to the bed, and I held on as he stuck two fingers in my pussy. I screamed out, but my breath was lost when he removed his fingers and plunged himself back into me.

Doggy style was a whole other feeling of pleasure. It allowed him to go as deep and hard as he wanted. I *loved* the control a man had over me from behind. His hands moved to my hips as he continued to fuck me.

One of his hands went underneath me to my chest where he was able to pull my back to him while keeping us locked together. My back was to his chest and as he continued to thrust into me, he kissed and licked my neck.

I heard him whisper something along the lines of I'm coming, but then, something unexplainable happened. I knew I was getting closer as he twitched inside of me, preparing to let himself go, but before I fell apart in his arms, I felt his mouth widen against my neck as he bit down, hard.

I cried out in what I wasn't sure was pain or pleasure. Immediately, the warmth I felt from him moments ago was gone. It was as if a bucket of ice cold water was poured on top of us. I quickly turned around to face him.

Something was weird, but I couldn't quite put my finger on it. He was turned away from me, and his shoulders were moving up and down in a fast paced motion. I got off the bed and went over to him, once I placed my hand on his shoulder though, was when he turned around and gave me a glimpse of who he really was.

A scream erupted from my throat.

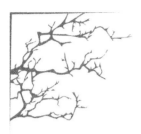

Chapter Six

M*ercy*

His eyes widened.

I backed away from him and ran. I didn't care that I was naked, all I knew was that I had to get out of there.

I didn't make it far. Strong arms wrapped around my waist and brought me back to the room that now felt like a prison.

Vampire.

I didn't think they existed. Sure, I've heard of mythologies based around them, like the television show Vampire Diaries and that book series Twilight, but never, did I ever think they were actually real.

He set me down on the bed, rather roughly I might add, and went to lock the door. I took that as the chance to escape out the window. He thought about that too. As soon as I plotted my escape and ran to the window, he was already there, blocking it. I looked to the other side of the bed and quickly rushed to the other window. Once again, he was already there.

He held his hands up. "Would you just stop for a minute?"

I shook my head and turned for the door. Somehow, he was there. Waiting for me. I lifted my hands in exasperation. "Let me leave!"

"No! You need to hear me out, Red."

I lifted my hands to my hair and screamed. "God, don't call me that! What was this, Cian? Were you trying to bring me back here so you could fuck me and then kill me? Are you insane?"

I sat on the bed and hunched over. I can't believe I actually let him...

My hand went to my mouth in horror. Tears started falling from my eyes. I just signed my own death warrant. How could I have been so stupid?

Black spots started to cloud my vision. I was on the verge of passing out. I knew it, and he obviously knew it because he was in front of me in the next second, trying to get me to breathe. I closed my eyes and willed myself to breathe in and out. I was able to gain control of my breathing again, but my heart was still racing.

I opened my eyes when Cian's hand went to my chin. I gave him a warning look and he dropped his hand immediately. His blue eyes roamed over my face. They were searching for something, but I couldn't put my finger on it. *Fear? Did he want to see me afraid of him? Afraid of what he was?*

My throat bobbed, maybe I *was* afraid of him. Afterall, there was so much to be scared of in the world now. *Murderers, serial killers, rapists, predators, sex traffickers. What the hell had I gotten myself into? What was I thinking?*

He ran a hand through his hair roughly and cursed.

33

A thought occurred to me, and I placed my hand on my neck to see if there was two bite marks imprinted in my skin. *That's weird. There's nothing there.* My brows turned inward. Maybe he didn't prick me? I thought I felt him bite me, I could've sworn I did.

"I didn't bite you, if that's what you're worried about."

My eyes snapped to his. "But I thought..."

He placed his hands on his naked hips. "I wanted to, believe me I did, but something stopped me."

My gaze roamed over him as I tried to look for any indication that he was, in fact, a vampire. Other than the fact that I saw his fangs when he turned around, he looked completely normal. No pale skin, no dark eyes, and he wasn't cold like I always thought they would be, like they were rumored to be.

I swallowed the lump in my throat. "So you're a..."

"A vampire? Yes."

I had a million questions, but the only thing that I could think of was, why hasn't he tried to kill me yet?

"Because I can't."

I looked away from the floor and back at him. "Huh?"

His blue eyes never left mine. "I can't kill you."

Did he just?

"No, I can't read your mind, but the question is written all over your face."

Oh, thank fuck for that.

I watched him closely as he turned away from me to go to his dresser. He pulled out a pair of shorts and put them on. Then he tossed something at me.

I caught it and noticed it was a long t-shirt.

"Put that on. If we're going to be having this conversation, I need some liquid courage."

I couldn't tell if he was mad or upset that I found out his secret. I honestly couldn't believe it myself. It all seemed so unreal.

I put the shirt on as he unlocked the bedroom door and walked out. I realized this was my opportune moment to escape, but for the life of me I couldn't do it anymore. Call it curiosity or stupidity, whatever it was, I wanted to know more.

I took a deep breath, stood up and walked out of the room and followed him to the kitchen.

Chapter Seven

M*ercy*

When I got to the kitchen, I saw him hovering over the counter in deep thought. The glass that had wine in it earlier was completely empty. Damn, he must have really needed that liquid courage.

He raised his head and his gaze met mine when I pulled out the bar stool and sat down. I waited for him to speak.

He poured more wine into the glass.

"Don't you want to be sober for this conversation?"

He set the wine bottle down, picked up the glass, and smirked. "It's not wine, Red."

My eyes widened. I stuttered. "You mean, that... that's..."

"Blood? Yes."

Wow, the surprises just kept on coming. I watched as he swallowed the thick liquid. "Don't you drink from humans?"

He set the glass down on the counter and placed his hands on the edges. He gave me his complete attention. "Yes."

Wow, one word answers. Helpful.

"The blood in the bottle is from a human. It's donated blood. As vampires, we don't usually prefer to drink from a package, but if there's no other choice, then we will do so to keep us alive." His eyes moved to my neck before they returned to my gaze. "Normally though, we prefer it to be warm and straight from the site."

Goosebumps arose on my arms, and I suddenly felt I was in danger.

"I won't hurt you. If I wanted to do that, I would've done so already."

He had a point.

My shoulders sagged in relief.

"Why aren't you cold to the touch? I thought vampires were cold blooded."

He backed away from the counter, reached into the fridge and handed me another bottle of water. I accepted it, took off the cap and swallowed a couple of sips. He leaned against the counter and crossed his arms. "There are a lot of myths about us. Technically, we are just like any normal human being. We can go out in sunlight, but we don't prefer to. We have normal skin temperature, and we eat real food just like you do, though we prefer blood. The only difference is, our senses are heightened. We can see, feel, and hear better than a human can. We can also have different powers depending on the vampire bloodline you come from. The more powerful your bloodline is, the more powerful you are, and so on."

As my brain tried to process all this my thoughts went to one thing. "What powers do you have?"

He shrugged. "It depends. Honestly, I'm still trying to figure all my powers out. I know I'm fast, and I can be invisible when I want to be."

Damn, that's incredible.

He was explaining all this to me but my brain only focused on one thing. Did I have an effect on him like he did to me? Or was it all one sided?

"Why did you pursue me at the bar? Was it for kicks? Were you trying to kill me? What was it?"

He pursed his lips. "I didn't go there to kill you. To be truthful, I didn't go there looking for anything. I was pissed off at my parents and decided to blow off some steam, and that's when I ran into you."

My heart started beating faster. "So, I was just a distraction?"

His gaze seared mine. "Yes."

"Oh." I whispered. Wow, all of a sudden I felt like gum stuck on the bottom of his shoe. I needed to get the fuck out of here. Who knew what his plans for me were now that I'd found out his secret?

I cleared my throat. "Well, it's been fun. I really should get going now." I stood up and tried to remember where the front door was. We came in from the garage door, but I remembered he already closed the garage before we entered the house.

"Mercy."

It wasn't often that he used my real name, so when he did, I looked up. "What?"

He swallowed. "Don't go."

There was something in his gaze, something that resembled vulnerability, but I knew I'd lost my mind. There was no way this man was vulnerable. No man was. Whatever I saw there prompted me to stay put.

"What do you want from me?" I asked, but it came out weaker than I planned.

He moved around the bartop until he was standing in front of me. I flinched and my eyes went to his face. *How did he do that?*

His hand tucked a piece of auburn hair behind my ear and stayed there. "I want you to stay."

He lifted my chin and placed a chaste kiss on my lips. He closed his eyes and rested his forehead against mine. "I want you to come upstairs, and help me finish where we left off."

His fingers moved to the base of my throat as he leaned back. I swallowed. "I want to taste you. Will you let me taste you? Will you let me devour you and make you completely mine?"

My heart dropped into my stomach. I closed my eyes as he leaned down to capture my lips. The kiss became heated as his fingers tangled in my hair, bringing me closer to him.

I realized in that moment that I'd do anything he'd ask.

I reached for the bottom of my shirt and started lifting it from my body. He got the memo and broke from my lips to get it off. Once the shirt was gone, he eagerly had his shorts off next. He moved my body to where he could gain access, and then he shoved inside. There was no foreplay this time as we dove straight for each other.

With each thrust he went deeper. He gathered my legs and wrapped them around his waist so he could take me harder. I wrapped my arms around him and held on. It felt so good, I never wanted him to stop.

"Fuck, Red. I'm getting close."

I was right on the edge with him, so when the next words came out of his mouth, I didn't hesitate to say yes.

"I want to bite you. I want to taste your fucking sweet as sin blood on my tongue. Tell me I can taste you, Red."

Another thrust.

He slid in and out of me, and I felt the familiar twitch. We were so close to going over the edge together.

"Yes," I whispered. My eyes rolled in the back of my head, and I leaned back so he could take what he wanted.

As he thrusted again, his tongue licked my neck and his fangs extended. I was already falling apart, and I *needed* him to be ready.

I screamed in pleasure when he bit down. My body convulsed against him, and my nails dug into his skin. Something warm and sticky poured down my neck as he continued to drink from me. My body became sluggish, and exhaustion began to creep in.

Finally, he came up for air and silenced my thoughts when he claimed my lips with his own. There was still blood on his mouth, so I was able to taste the metal as his tongue tangled with mine. Every time I'd gotten a chapped lip or bitten my lip in the past, blood always tasted like metal. I used to think it was gross, but when it came from his lips, I didn't give a damn.

I grew wet again, and while he was still inside me, he went hard. I knew that with this man, it would be impossible to tear myself from him. One taste, and I was addicted.

We fucked all night until we both finally became exhausted.

It wasn't until I woke up the next morning with a full heart and soul full of possibilities that I hadn't considered before, to having the most painful and gut wrenching realization. I was utterly the stupidest human on planet fucking earth for falling into his trap.

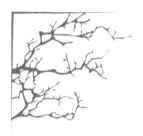

Chapter Eight

M*ercy*

I was brought out of the flashback when a familiar hand was placed on my shoulder. His concerned eyes never left mine. I swallowed the lump in my throat and took a few steps back, leaving his hand to fall to his side.

He ran a hand through his short hair and cursed under his breath. My stomach was twisted in knots as I waited to hear what he would say. Did I want to hear what he had to say though? He left me two years ago today, and now all of a sudden he shows up?

Why didn't he explain why he left? How could a person do that after the night we had, after the promises he made to me?

The tears threatened to leak from my eyes. This was why I didn't do relationships. This was why I didn't get involved with men at all. I kept to my studies and focused on nothing else. Men only left a trail of pain and heartache, and the honest truth was, I didn't need any more of that in my life.

"What are you doing here?" My voice came out hoarse and broken. I wanted to sound strong and confident, like his leaving didn't break me to my fucking core. But, I couldn't. After that night we had two years ago, when I gave myself to him and let him see all of the demons that threatened to destroy me on a day to day basis, I knew I couldn't hide from him. Even though I wanted to.

His gaze returned to mine. He seemed to be struggling with what he wanted to say. I knew Chloe was worried. The problem was, Cian had this power that made him invisible if he wanted to be. I knew he wanted to be invisible to Chloe because he didn't want to deal with the repercussions that would follow.

All of a sudden, determined eyes replaced the hesitant and concerned ones I saw a moment ago. His jaw ticked as he stood taller, and his hands clenched at his sides. *There he was.* This was the vengeful vampire prince I knew he was down to his core. He took a step closer, and that caused my heart to race.

"I'm taking you home."

My brows turned inward. "Home? I am home, Cian."

He removed the hood from his head, causing him to be revealed to the world and Chloe. I heard her gasp behind me.

"I'm taking you to my home, Little Red."

I glared and gripped the strings on my backpack tighter. I shook my head. "I'm not going anywhere with you, Cian. You don't own me. You didn't then, and you certainly don't now."

I turned away from him and went to my last class of the day when he whispered the words that stopped me in my tracks.

"You're my mate, Red."

To be continued...

Thank you for reading Mercy and Cian's story, Innocent Promise! This was the prequel to my Dark Vampire Romance Trilogy Entitled The Promise Trilogy. Their story will be continued in A Vampire's Promise Releasing Fall 2024. If you would like to receive updates about their trilogy and my other books, visit me on my website: www.authorharperray.com

About the Author

As an author of dark romance, Harper has a passion for writing stories that readers enjoy reading over and over again. Her imagination is the creative tool that helps her come up with several intriguing storylines that she hopes to share with the world. Her fans call her the "page turner author" because with each story she sucks the readers in, instantly hooking them from page one.

Harper loves to read books of all kinds but romance is her favorite. She's also a first grade elementary school teacher, recently got married to her husband, has two dogs named Twigg and Cricket, and a cat named Skipper. Harper and her husband are hoping to expand their small little family soon!

Printed in Great Britain
by Amazon